Edited by Valerie Sweeten

ISBN-13: 978-1981276158

ISBN-10:1981276157

Ramses & The Great Wonder

By

T.L. Johnson

To my great wonder T.J.

Love always

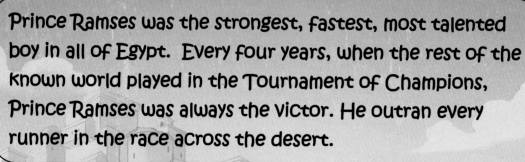

Prince Ramses was the strongest, fastest, most talented boy in all of Egypt. Every four years, when the rest of the known world played in the Tournament of Champions, Prince Ramses was always the victor. He outran every runner in the race across the desert.

He jumped higher than everyone
in the high jump.

And his strength was unmatched when he threw his javelin.

The other nations became frustrated, competing against Ramses, because they never won. Eventually, the nations stopped sending their athletes to the Games.

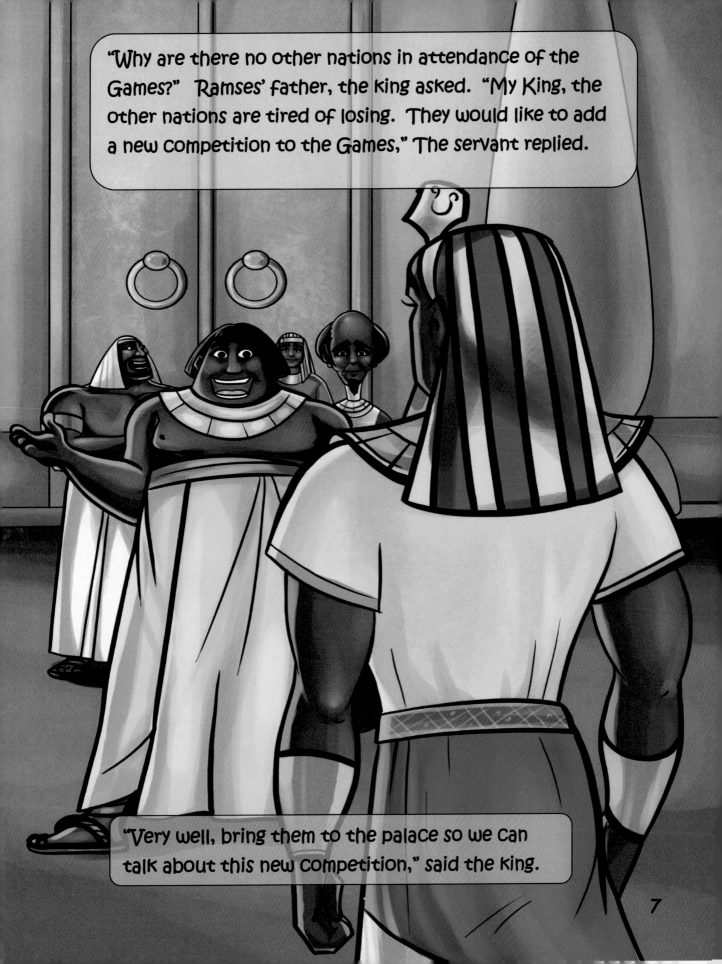

"Why are there no other nations in attendance of the Games?" Ramses' father, the king asked. "My King, the other nations are tired of losing. They would like to add a new competition to the Games," The servant replied.

"Very well, bring them to the palace so we can talk about this new competition," said the king.

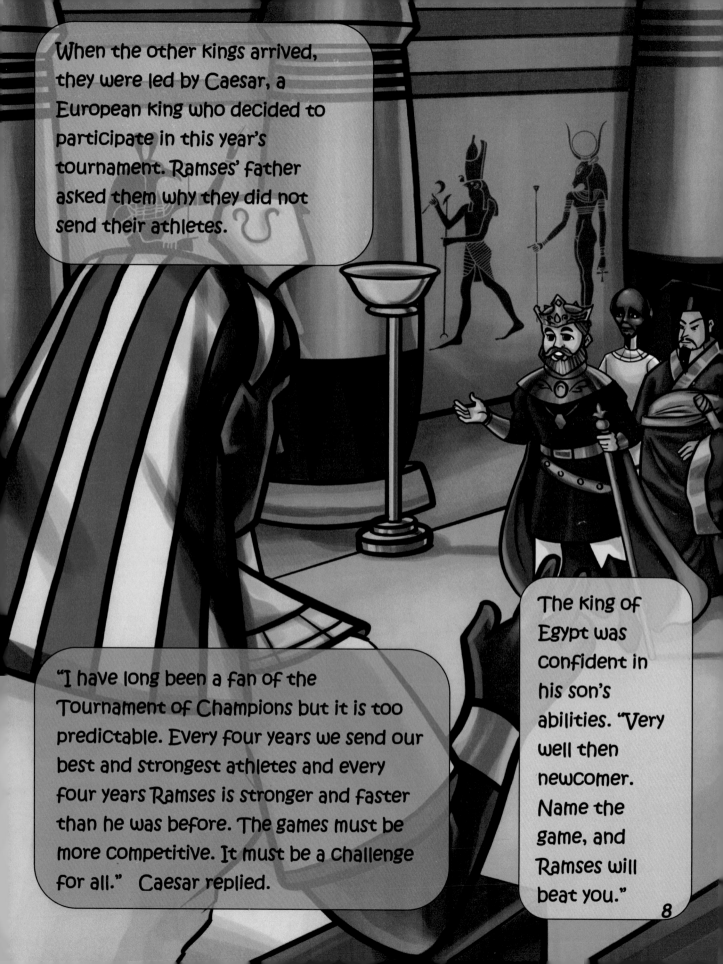

When the other kings arrived, they were led by Caesar, a European king who decided to participate in this year's tournament. Ramses' father asked them why they did not send their athletes.

"I have long been a fan of the Tournament of Champions but it is too predictable. Every four years we send our best and strongest athletes and every four years Ramses is stronger and faster than he was before. The games must be more competitive. It must be a challenge for all." Caesar replied.

The king of Egypt was confident in his son's abilities. "Very well then newcomer. Name the game, and Ramses will beat you."

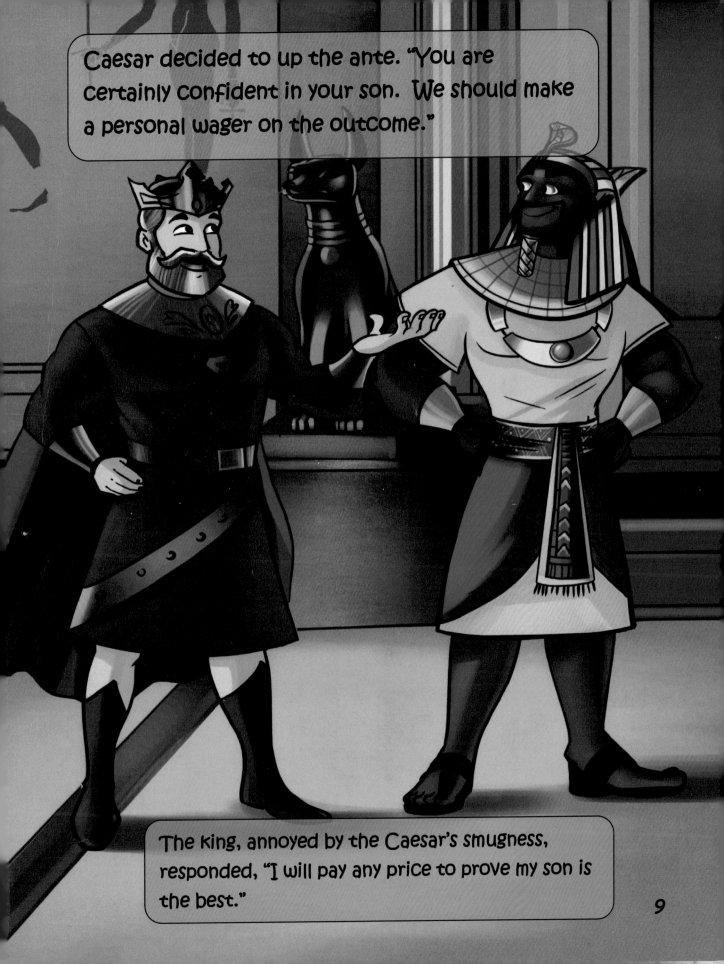

Caesar decided to up the ante. "You are certainly confident in your son. We should make a personal wager on the outcome."

The king, annoyed by the Caesar's smugness, responded, "I will pay any price to prove my son is the best."

"If we win," said Caesar, "you must surrender your land and your people to be ruled by us."

The king laughed. "I accept this challenge. It is a foolish bet, but I will agree. Now, what if I win?"

Caesar said, "If your son defeats us. We will give you the Emerald of Tatyana. The most prized gem in our nation."

The king responded boastfully, "You have nothing I want. Ramses will compete only to show the world that he is the greatest in the world."

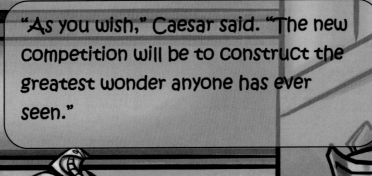

"As you wish," Caesar said. "The new competition will be to construct the greatest wonder anyone has ever seen."

The king was shocked. "That is not an athletic event!"

"No one said it had to be. You have eight days to build something the world has never seen before," said Caesar with a smirk.

Ramses ran out of the palace. He ran until he could no longer see it. He sat there for hours, alone, but he could not think of a great wonder the world had never seen.

Just then, the strangers pulled back their hoods! Before Ramses stood Ra, Horus and Isis; the original rulers of their land. Before him stood three powerful, ancient kings!

"Ramses, you are by far the most physically gifted person we ever created, but you refuse to use your most powerful muscle." The kings told him.

"But, I use all my muscles," He replied.

It was then the kings revealed to Ramses what his most important gift was that he possessed.

"It is true that you run faster than anyone else, you jump higher than anyone else, and you throw the javelin farther than anyone else, but none of those muscles will design a great wonder. No, your most powerful muscle is your mind. Train this muscle like you do your body, and you will think quicker than anyone else. That is how you will win."

This truth inspired Ramses. "Of course! My mind is a muscle, too. I just have to train it. Thank you so much!"

"Now, go save your kingdom, Prince Ramses," The kings commanded.

With that, he ran back to the kingdom to work on his wonder.

19

Next, they traveled to Rome. "As you can see, we have the greatest wonder in the world," said Caesar, proudly displaying the Leaning Tower of Pisa.

All the kings agreed this was indeed the best wonder—everyone but the Egyptian king.

"I must admit this is impressive, but the completion isn't over until we see what my son has built. " They all agreed and traveled to Egypt.

When they arrived, Caesar felt confident he had won. "Where is your wonder?" He asked in a very confident tone.

The king of Egypt shrugged his shoulders, prepared to admit defeat.

Suddenly, Ramses appeared.

"There is my wonder!" The king shouted looking at his son.

"Sorry I am late, but if you follow me, I will show you the wonder I have built," Ramses said.

Rising out of the desert was the most marvelous structure the world had ever seen.

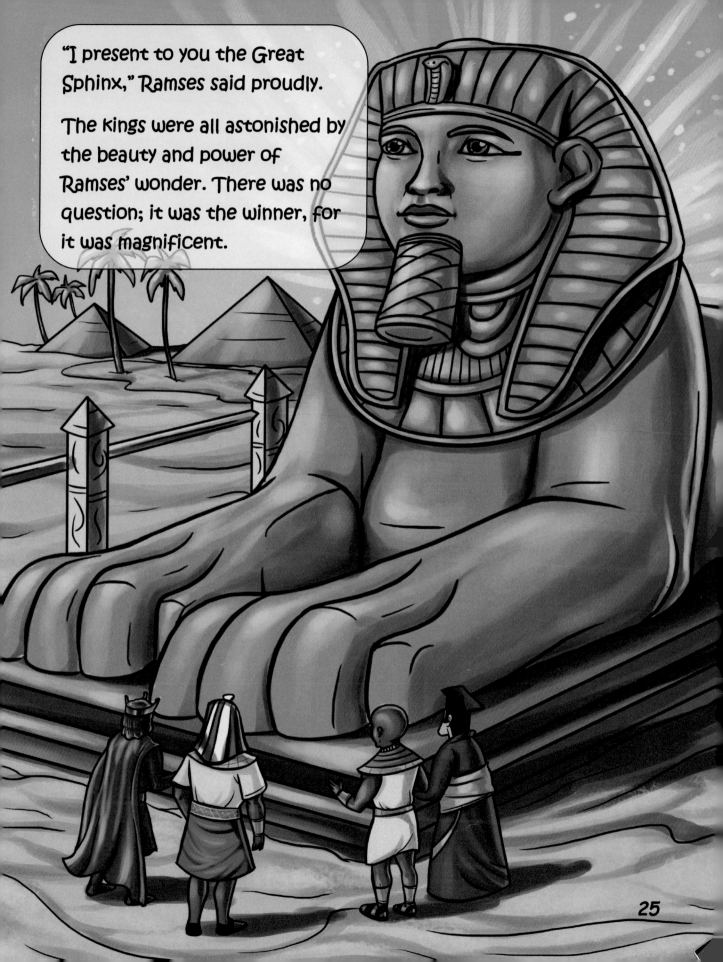

"This truly is the greatest wonder in the world," said the Chinese emperor.

"I must agree," said Caesar. "I have never ever seen anything like it in all my travels."

The king of Egypt looked at his son.

"Ramses, you have done the incredible. How did you do this?"

"I realized that while I have been gifted with powerful muscles, the most powerful muscle is my mind. So, I used it," he replied.

The delighted king hugged his son.

"Ramses, you are going to make a great leader someday, and you are right. If you use your mind, you will always create great wonders."

- End